Gymkitasaurus©

You'll never leave your Gym
kit in school again!!

For everyone that forgets their gym kit young and old and those who have to put the stinky items in the wash!!

Chapter One

The sun danced on strings of light and kissed Tristyn's cheek; it was a beautiful sunny day in April and Tristyn was enjoying his snooze. He did not hear his alarm or his mum calling him to wake up, it was already well past nine o'clock and he had no intention of moving until midday.

It was the first proper day of half term, not the Saturday and Sunday before that make you think it's the half term then mum informs you there are still swimming lessons!! Oh no! This

was a proper day, it was Monday
and Tristyn intended to stay
wrapped up in his bed-fort looking
out across the room with one
solitary eye trying to decide if he
was looking at a fly on the wall or
was it in fact a piece of fluff?
"Tristyn get up", Mum's yelling fell
on deaf ears, he was not moving
that was final! Now back to the
fluff or fly, (he still hadn't decided)

WHOOSH!! Tristyn's bedroom
door flew open and there stood
mum. She was an opposing sort of
lady, 5 foot 8 inches tall and
rather rotund, (i.e. bulbous around
the middle, i.e. a little on the

cuddly side, i.e. overweight but don't ever tell her that or she'll shoot you the look, you know the one that can make baby minitour's cry and great white sharks give up swimming forever). She was wearing pink washing up gloves with frilly edges and an apron that said "Happy" on it – she however did not look happy at all, she looked like the most-windy of rainy days wrapped in a blanket of itchy pips. That's right MIS..ER..AB..LE!!

Before Tristyn could even think about why he hadn't heard her running up the stairs, she had opened her mouth to shout. Having felt the verbal fury of the mum monster on previous lazy days, Tristyn decided to hop out of bed, "I am just getting up mum, I did hear you", "Good", mum smiled, "Hurry up and come on down for breakfast".

Sulking Tristyn threw on his slippers and slopped down the stairs for breakfast. He was not a happy bunny and he was not getting dressed – not yet anyway!

Tristyn walked slowly down the stairs still in his train PJ's and now wearing his ninja slippers. Mum had managed to get him out of bed but today was going to be a lazy day. He had no plans; no cycling, no football, no swimming, nothing! It was just going to be him, the TV and the bag of 'cinema night' treats – bliss! Well at least that was the plan.

Chapter Two

Mathuw and Ieuan were already sitting at the table FULLY DRESSED!!! There was not a ninja slipper in sight – not one! Well apart from the two that Tristyn was wearing but they didn't count. "Oh, good morning Tristyn", sang out Dad and his brothers all sitting there like annoying little gnomes, they had all been in this position before, the last one down to breakfast was never a good position to be in, usually it meant getting told off for being late for school but not today, it was half term and Tristyn was very confident it would all be fine. "Did you have a good sleep?" Mum asked very pleasantly, almost too pleasantly, "Yes, yes I did mum" said the ever-suspicious super sleuth – why was mum being so nice this morning, what did she have planned? "That's good", mum said smiling as she topped up dad's cup of tea, then he noticed it, everyone's coats were lined up on the back of the sofa and shoes and trainers were lined up in the hall. "Where is everyone going?" Tristyn asked not really wanting to hear the answer, "We have to go shopping today for some new school shoes for all of you", mum said smiling! Yes, she was smiling – she knew everyone hated going shopping and she was pinching one of their holiday days to go, how mean! Tristyn's young heart shouted out a silent and ominous, "NOOOOOOO!!!!!!!!!" as his lazy plans melted away to nothingness!! He would not be able to laze about and watch TV while scratching himself; he would not be able to gorge on the cinema night treats while flicking through the kids channels; he would not be able to flick the empty sweet papers across the room trying to get them into the bin. All the sweets had to stay in their wrappers as he had to go out SHOPPING!!! What a *GREAT* start to the half term!!! "What, why, when was this decided then?"

Tristyn was very confused what with being still a little bit tired, he decided that he may still be dreaming – yes! That was it, he was in fact dreaming, his illusions were shattered when his mum roared out, "Oi! Mr Grumpy! We are going shopping this morning because you all need new shoes and I'm only off today and tomorrow and I want to go to the park tomorrow as the weather is going to be better. This was all decided this morning while you were still sleeping, if you can't be bothered to come down to breakfast and be here when everyone else is making decisions don't think that you can then make a fuss about them. Is that OK with you?!". Tristyn really struggled not to answer mum back but the look on her face just told him that he didn't need to bother to answer back, the decision was made and that was that.

Tristyn sat at the breakfast table and chose his cereal, half a bowl of sugar squares and half a bowl

of puffy Choco rice; that was
another lesson learnt .....

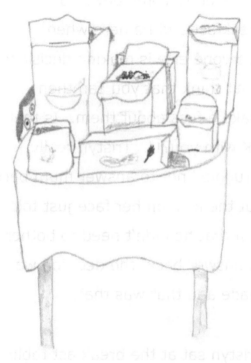

NEVER ask mum for more variety
of cereal when we are in a rush in
the supermarket then try and back

pedal and say you just fancy toast the very next day!!!!

The whole family were now munching their way through no less than **EIGHT** opened boxes of cereal and no-one dare tell mum they had had enough of cereal and just wanted fruit juice or a smoothie.

Tristyn poured his milk into the bowl and Started to eat just as Dad finished off his tea and caught his eye, "What?" Tristyn asked his Dad indignantly, "Tristyn, oh Tristyn, do you notice anything hanging on the line?" Dad asked as he waved his hand towards the patio door. Tristyn leaned over to his left giving a small huff while rolling his eyes for he knew what was coming next, "Yes Dad, I can see people's gym kits on the washing line – Ewww! Even their stinky old daps!!" Tristyn sat back down feeling very pleased with himself and his witty reply, "That's right Tristyn – People's gym kits. Mathuw and Ieuan's gym kits to be precise but not yours, in fact yours is nowhere in sight again, can you tell me why that is?"

Tristyn felt the heat of Mum's gaze in the back of his head, he knew he was going to be in trouble, this was the third time he had forgotten his gym kit this year! He decided it was best he tell a fib, "It was Miss Williams' fault, she didn't give me my gym kit to bring home, what could I do? I'm a child after all"; Tristyn hoped that his answer was just believable enough without being cheeky that it would stop any more questions. He was so wrong, like a hungry dog, mum was straight on the conversation. She was icing on a birthday cake a very cross very shouty birthday cake, "Did you give Miss Williams the letter I gave you specifically to give to her? It begged her to send your gym kit home with you, it told her you hadn't brought your gym kit home the last two holidays!". Mum was visibly puzzled and seemed a little more agitated than previous times Tristyn had forgotten to bring his gym kit home. Why was she so agitated, what was so different this time compared to other times? Tristyn had no choice but to continue with his fib he was too far committed now, he just hoped Mum did not look in his bag because she would see straight away that he was fibbing!! "Yes, Mum I did", Tristyn said while crossing his toes and his fingers on his right side, he began shoveling cereal into his mouth hoping beyond hope that mum would not find out that he had forgotten to give Miss Williams the letter AGAIN!

"That's not like Miss Williams to ignore my letters but anyway Tristyn your kit is your responsibility you need to start remembering to bring it home for washing – it's dangerous if you don't!"

Chapter Three

The three boys and dad sat at the
table glued to their chairs, they
had stopped in their tracks,
mouths a little open but none
wanting to ask the question –
Then the silence was broken,
Mathuw couldn't resist anymore
"What are you on about mum?" he
asked not daring to move a
muscle in his face in case he
showed the wrong emotion and
Mum let out a shriek like a
banshee and engulfed him whole,
(she wouldn't have done it really
but would you take the risk?) Mum
seemed to crumple up like a crisp

packet as she studied Mathuw's face for signs of a smile or a frown, what was he thinking. When she had decided that he wasn't going to let her know whether he was laughing at her or not she visibly relaxed which made Mathuw heave a sigh of relief he had faced the Mum monster and won – YES!!, but he made a mistake he thought he was being a gentleman and reminding mum she had not finished her sentence, "Mum you were saying" but it reawakened the Mum monster, "No, Don't worry about it, forget I said anything", Mum said very quickly and a little more defensively than she intended.

There was a second's silence then Mathuw plucked up the courage to ask the fabled question again, he wanted to know, and he knew his brothers and Dad wanted to know as well they were all just a bit chicken, "Sorry mum, what do you mean it's dangerous?" Mum sighed, "OK I'll tell you, but you must not laugh! Well when I was a little girl there was a girl a few years older than me, she never took her gym kit home, in fact there were quite a few children in my school who were the same,

when we got to the third half term
in the school year something
dreadful happened. Luckily for me
Nanny Sha made sure we always
took our gym kit home." Mathuw
looked at mum puzzled, "So how
was that dangerous then mum?",
"I'm getting to that bit!" Mum
said getting a little flustered. She
didn't really want to say anything,
she knew they would laugh but
they needed to know the truth.
"Anyway, this half term the rancid
old gym kits came to life and
totally destroyed the school! They
painted with all the paints in the
art rooms, sewed all the netball
and football kits together in

textiles and even burnt down our science labs!! I'm not sure why or how it happened, I just know it did and we had to rebuild the whole school it was wrecked!. It took months which meant we had to work in porta cabins! I have thought about it a lot over the years and I can only think that it must have been the sheer stink, it made the fibres come to life or something."

The boys sat deathly still, no-one daring to breathe for fear a cascade of laughter would spill from them and no-one wanted to be the boy who laughed when mum was still looking so serious. Tristyn foolishly decided to take a big gulp of breath and that was it! He lost all composure erupting laughter all over the table top and infecting them all with the chuckle wave. Little laughs spiraled to huge booming, 'can't breathe properly' roars – everyone was affected!! Everyone that was except for mum who was still looking incredibly serious about the whole matter, "I'm only saying what I heard, the school was wrecked!!", silence fell over the room then the laughter started again, "Why have you never told me this story before, it's hilarious!" Dad asked his face going slightly crimson from the laughter. "This, this is why", Mum said motioning to the table with her hands, "I'm serious boys, imagine how you would feel if your school gets trashed by your gym kit!" That was the limit, Dad exploded into a huge snort laughter hurricane and swept the boys up with him they all laughed so much that by the time they finished their sides were sore, "Don't believe me then" said mum with a smile for she finally saw the funny side, "I realise it sounds ridiculous but don't be surprised if Mr James has to do some disaster

management and all your gym kits
have been burnt or put into a
stinky black bag.

Chapter Four

What the boys and Dad didn't know though, was just how close to the truth Mum was for inside Newcity Primary school something very strange was happening indeed. Outside the Butterfly classroom on Tristyn's peg, the navy-blue gym bag with the golden apple tree logo had started to swell. Just like an infected boil it grew and grew, swelling to three times its original size. Inside the bag the stinky gym kit swam around in the rancid stench of three half terms worth of sweat mud and general grossness, it began gaining strength from the foul pong. Just when the gym bag swelled to breaking point, a force from inside pushed the pull cord open. The gaping mouth of the bag grew wider and an acrid green cloud of despair and pong started to seep out onto the floor below. The green mist cloud was so putrid that anything it touched instantly became animated moving all by itself; every unpaired sock, lonely wellington boot and seasonally confused woolen hat started moving around the floor without reason or purpose, then IT emerged!

From inside Tristyn's bag, an armless sleeve poked slowly through the gaping drawstring mouth surrounded by plumes of the acrid, green mist cloud which flowed freely onto the floor like a fresh waterfall on a crisp autumn day. There was a spray that accompanied the mist, it was commanding jets of steam, like a water-gun and sending stinking green droplets splashing onto the surrounding pegs and remnants of clothing. It was not enough to animate them properly, so they just wiggled about like a slow slithering slug on a grassy verge. A few larger pieces of clothing had been bathed in the mists and were moving around autonomously. Seeing that the other clothing was struggling to come to life the clothing began to drag down the odd coats and scarves that had been left on pegs bathing them in the mists on the floor creating a coaty, beasty thing.

The sleeve in Tristyn's gym bag continued to push through, being born to a new world, like an eyeless lizard it moved from side to side looking for a way down to the floor, slowly the neck, second sleeve and very crumpled, very stinky body dragged itself from

the bag and the stench ridden T
Shirt stood triumphantly on the
edge of its bagged prison,
surveying the carnage that was
ensuing below.

Very carefully the T shirt started
to make its way down the side of
the bag before SPLAT!! It hit the

floor with a thump, next came the shorts hitting the floor with a louder splat, closely followed by two daps that slithered down gracefully like two ends of a very weird cobra. The tongues wrapped around each other like rose bud petals and the little laces grappled around the bag strings like spaghetti fingers, they slowly began aiding to lower the daps to the floor.

Now because Tristyn had not brought his gym kit home for a long time, each half term mum sent him back in with a fresh kit, which he just added to the bag.

He used each set intermittently depending on how much each one smelled at any one time; because of this several more pieces of gym kit fell out of Tristyn's bag onto the floor where they began to mingle and mix with remnants of gym kits from Tristyn's classmates and those of other classes that had come wandering across to pair up. Tristyn's gym kit started to move into position, T-Shirt at the top followed by shorts then daps at the bottom with football socks hanging behind the daps like two little tails. With one jump the gymkitosaurus stood upright, the size of a medium dog and blindly looked across the cloakroom, it was as though it could see what was going on but how could it, it had no eyes after all. Maybe it used a sort of stink-echo a bit like a bat or a dolphin using echolocation, the gymkitosaurus was using stinklocation. All we know is that Tristyn's gymkitosaurus, (that's a mouthful we can call it T Gymkitosaurus from now on), started to move, in the direction of Butterfly classroom ready to wreak some havoc!

With one slide of the door, it was inside and ready to get started!!

As T gymkitosaurus walked into
the room the stinky green gas
above his gaping neckline seemed
to become a wide wicked smile
and even a face seemed to form
making him look even more
menacing, he was quickly followed
in by others of all shapes and
sizes. Why was it a he you ask?
Well the male stench from
Tristyn's sweaty gym kit had male
DNA in it, skin cells and as a result
created a male gymkitasaurus,
female gym kits and sweat made
female gymkitasaurus's.
Some of T gymkitasurus's new
friends were not as well made,
they had two T shirts or two pairs

of shorts, one even had two T shirts and NO SHORTS!! Imagine the embarrassment!

When in the classroom the gymkitasaurus's or should that be gymkitasauri? Anyway, they all started to empty carefully labelled boxes of classroom supplies onto the floor. The rulers were no longer in their box, the wooden blocks were in a pile in the middle of the carpet, making a mockery of carefully placed labels, then it saw it!

T gymkitosaurus saw the craft table, it let out a low moan of enthusiasm as it sloped across the room to begin its work. Glitter and glue and foamy shapes flew through the air in a flurry of destruction – What a mess!!!! T gymkitasaurus stayed in Miss Williams's room for over an hour just doing really naughty things, it scribbled on the front of all the children's workbooks, put all the farm animals in the zoo and jumbled up the shop with the mud kitchen!! The horror!!

Happy that it had made a suitable mess in Miss Williams's Butterfly classroom, T gymkitasaurus decided to walk into the corridor where it let out a squeal of pleasure, (no-one knows how or why it was able to squeal with pleasure, I've asked everyone like my nan and she's really old! Perhaps it was the stench clouds bashing together?), for so much mayhem was afoot, it would make your hair curl. Reading books were being used as frisbee's, the cosy corner looked like a catastrophe!! The writing table was being used as a barricade as naughty gymkitasari were holding an epic paint and crepe paper battle across the hallway. T gymkitasaurus happily joined in the carnage and was solely responsible for turning the year two, yard windows into a mixture of purple, pink and gold paint and glitter, it was almost artistic if it wasn't so messy. The glittery painty mess rolled down the windows and pooled on the floor like a sticky skating rink, the glitter really made it shine! The baby gymkitasaurusi from the reception and nursery classes were making paint and glitter angels in the ever-growing puddle that was spreading farther and farther across the floor, they looked like little paint brushes as they coloured the hall carpet – what fun!

Chapter Five

Acting almost like a supervisor, T gymkitasaurus decided it would walk around the school and take part in all the chaos; it stuck all the sea creature toys to the ceiling in the wide mouth frog room, pulled all the keys off the keyboards in the computer room and used the heads of the dolls from the ladybird room to paint all the chairs in the year three classrooms.   T gymkitasaurus decided it was time to look in on the older junior classrooms but looking down the corridor there were just too many gymkitasauri!!

A huge fight had started among them over the cooking trolley and two of the largest gymkitasauri had amassed a large gathering as they climbed on top of it, where they engaged in a wrestling match to see which group would gain ownership of the trolley and the cooking utensils within – what a prize! The gymkitasauri were much more aggressive and the sheer numbers was crazy, perhaps it was because more pupils in years three and above had forgotten to take their gym kits home?

T gymkitasaurus decided to go into the canteen for that was the next door it came to. In the canteen a huge gymkitasaurus had taken charge and was commanding armies of smaller gymkitasauri in a game of flour tag. Bags and bags of flour flew across the room and exploded in mid-air creating huge floury clouds that also took on a green tint as the stench engulfed them. The particles danced around in the air fighting for the space like dust when acting in Brownian motion. T gymkitasaurus joined in the mayhem on the edge of the game then suddenly things got a little more dangerous as one of the bigger gymkitasauri brought out cartons of fruit juice and began to throw these across the canteen as well!

These did not explode in the air like the flour bags whose particles were still fighting for dominance in mid-air, it was quite beautiful to watch but ooh so messy! The cartons flew in a straight line across the canteen then exploded on the floor. Liquid droplets, rolled across the floor like a million marbles and started to gloop together creating an apple-orange wave.

Very soon and without warning the flour had gathered together and stopped fighting for space instead it amassed to a floury cloud that was trying to escape into the hall to go and destroy something else. The liquid then took on a movement of its own and began lapping at the doors like the sea. T gymkitasaurus decided to leave this room before a tsunami developed and engulfed them all!! As T gymkitasarus moved past the biggest gymkitasaurus a name tag could be seen on the inside out T Shirt it read, 'Mr Thomas'!! Oh dear! even Mr Thomas had forgotten to take home his gym kit this half term.

The doorway back out into the corridor was now blocked by the flour cloud that had realised if it floated low enough it could get

through the door and it was all
trying to escape, it started to
swarm around some rouge
gymkitasauri that were trying to
get out and was picking them up
and carrying them high into the
air, leaving them in the rafters,
that way was no good.

The outside of the building was
locked shut and there were
already several gymkitasaurus's
trying to open the door, so T
gymkitasaurus went through the
only door available even though it
was unthinkable, the door to the
offices.

Chapter Six

Stood by the front door was Dewi the school dragon, he was looking out through the front door protecting the school from outside threats, who would have thought the school would be destroyed from within?

To most of the children, parents, staff and visitors to the school, Dewi was little more than a statue the school had adopted as their mascot. The school had raised funds to buy the Dewi from a local art shop and he fit right in at the school with his bright red back and green belly he was a sight to behold! But Dewi was so much more than just a plaster statue! Dewi was the school's protector. From the day he entered the school he was washed by the magic and mystery of the school and a magical spell was placed on him. The spell ensured that when the time arose, and the school is at threat, Dewi becomes incarnated, (that means he comes to life!), in full dragon form.

This was one such time when the unique spell that kept him glued to his plinth was lifted.

As the plumes of green naughtiness were wafting underneath the door into the entrance hall where Dewi stood, like a light switch, the spell was activated.

Slowly Dewi's bright red scales glowed and popped as the heat of his internal firepit came to life. Little puffs of white smoke spilled from his mouth and slowly his lower jaw started to stretch and move with a crunching and grinding.

As more and more of his body came to life, Dewi started to make a low growling noise, he was getting ready to do his job. Once his body had warmed from inside like a kiln and he could move his toes he jumped off his plinth and stood claw-footed on the carpet. With a shriek and lots of flapping he quickly jumped back on his plinth, he had never felt carpet before and it felt weird!!

After a few seconds of self-motivation Dewi made the leap onto the carpet again, this time standing tall and straight ready to take on this naughtiness. It was the first time he had been called into action and he was determined to do a good job.

T gymkitasaurus had been stood behind the heavy velvet curtains that had been pulled across the front door watching Dewi come to life. When he saw Dewi jump back onto the plinth like a spring rabbit, he decided this dragon was not going to be a threat and sneaked past him. Unfortunately for him, he was not familiar with the school layout and as he tried to slip into what he thought was the office or headteachers room he took a wrong turn and ran straight into the medical room! T gymkitosaurus let out a low grumble and seemed to shake his cloud head for being so foolish, confident that the dragon had not seen him and sure he was still fighting with his carpet phobia, T gymkitosaurus thought it was going to get away without being seen. Unfortunately for him, he made another mistake and fell over his own feet as he backed out of the room, bumping straight into the box of unclaimed water bottles which sent them crashing to the floor and he wailed in what appeared to be pain but how could it be pain he wasn't real!

There was a low rumble and creaking as Dewi instantly looked towards the medical room and saw all the bottles flying out through the doorway, he knew something was not right, empty rooms do not moan, and water bottles do not fly about by themselves. Bravely he turned and started to walk; (like a kitten with a tissue on its paws; that walky, flicky, jumpy walk, he still wasn't overly keen on the carpet); into the medical room.

T gymkitasaurus heard Dewi walking towards the room and had to choose to fight him and probably lose; or hide. He decided it was too dangerous to try and leave so T gymkitasaurus hid in the corner and waited for Dewi. As Dewi began to walk into the room T Gymkitasaurus ran

underneath him knowing that
Dewi would not be able to turn
very easily, although he had come
to life he was still a plaster
dragon. Quickly T gymkitasaurus
pushed past Dewi and left him in
the room facing the wrong way!
Poor Dewi! he was stuck fast and
T gymkitasaurus just locked him
in! Who would save the school
now?

With Dewi safely out of the way T
gymkitasaurus turned to the front
office, he opened the door and
saw the piles of letters and
notebooks and handwriting pens
and again he roared with pleasure!

Immediately he started to throw all the paperwork off the desks onto the floor and danced all over them, kicking them into the air; they fell back down to earth like snow covered Autumn leaves. T gymkitasaurus had such fun throwing around lunch money envelopes, photocopying his stinky shoe and licking all the windows with his newly formed tongue but he became bored very quickly. After dancing in the paper leaves he decided he would go to the most forbidden room in the school, Mrs Ploughy's office …..

Chapter Seven

While utter carnage was being reeked in the school, Tristyn and his family were busy shopping for new shoes, "Come on Tristyn be a bit more enthusiastic about this will you?", Dad teased, "Buying shoes is so thrilling!"

Just as Tristyn was about to have a truly epic strop and start throwing himself about in an attempt to get sent back to the car to 'cool off' – result!, he stopped suddenly and gave a huge fake smile then froze to the spot like a mouse smelling the scent of the neighbourhood cat as he heard a voice he recognized; "Tristyn, I hope you are enjoying your holidays". Tristyn turned around to see Miss Williams carrying what seemed like a million shopping bags, she was with Mrs Ploughy. Nervously Tristyn looked around to see if he could find his mum she was looking at some hand-crafted love spoons – phew. "Hi Miss Williams, do you remember you ... um you didn't give me my gym kit even though I gave you the letter from Mummy?" Tristyn spoke so fast he almost fell over his words. Miss Williams looked puzzled, "What letter?" Before Tristyn could start to explain what the letter had contained and try to convince Miss Williams that he had in fact given it to her; even though he knew he hadn't and it was just a fib that was going so horribly wrong; (Why did teachers have to go shopping anyway?); Mum appeared behind him, "Ah Miss Williams, did Tristyn give you a letter asking for you to send home his gym kit, it's been three holidays now and he hasn't brought it home".

"What?!" Shouted Mrs Ploughy a little too loudly making everyone jump, "Oh sorry Mrs Clemett, did you say that Tristyn has not brought his gym kit home for three holidays now?", "That's right, he hasn't, why?" Mrs Ploughy suddenly turned very pale, "Don't worry it's fine, I feel a little tired now Miss Williams we had better go", Miss Williams looked very confused, it was not like Mrs Ploughy to be so rude and interrupt her before she could even answer Tristyn's mum's question, she stared directly at Mrs Ploughy who looked like a rabbit in the headlights. "So boys are you enjoying your holiday?" Miss Williams said completely mis-reading Mrs Ploughy's non-verbal que to leave. Tristyn did a small victory dance as the conversation was quickly moved on from his mum's question, he was going to get away with this!

Mrs Ploughy could see that she needed to speed things up so she started to groan and hold her side, "Oh my side, all this walking has really hurt my side, I need to go home – now", "Oh, OK Mrs Ploughy I have walked my feet off anyway" Miss Williams said as she turned to see Mrs Ploughy skulking off in the direction of the car, "I'm sorry we had to leave so suddenly, enjoy the rest of your holidays boys and no Mrs Clemett Tristyn didn't give me any letter about a gym kit". With that Miss Williams and Mrs Ploughy left the shops and disappeared into the carpark.

"Mrs Ploughy why do we need to leave so early? I know that you have not hurt your side you almost ran across the carpark!" Miss Williams asked as they reached the car, "Because if Tristyn has left his gym kit there again for the third time, this could be very bad for the school".

Tristyn's mum looked a little shocked for a few minutes, she was not used to people not answering her properly then just walking away before she could question them or Tristyn on why he had fibbed about giving Miss Williams the letter. Mum was thankfully for Tristyn, lost in thought, "Why was Mrs Ploughy so worried about Tristyn's gym kit? I bet that my story is true! What if your gym kit ruins your school Tristyn", "No! Not our school" shouted the boys in unison.

Mum was just about to race after Mrs Ploughy when she suddenly became faint and needed to sit down. Seeing that Mum was a little shell-shocked Dad decided to announce, "Last shop so we have to buy shoes here then we'll go for pizza before going home to have a cinema night" With a new-found enthusiasm for shoe buying fueled by the promise of pizza, the boys went to the next shop and all got their shoes in the first few minutes. They behaved so well they also got a packet of football cards for their collection. That night they all chose the film, "Monster school" so everything was wonderful. Mum didn't even remember to speak to Tristyn; (we all know that means shout at with her pointy finger wagging); for fibbing about giving Miss Williams the letter.

What Tristyn did not know, was that Mrs Ploughy had dropped Miss Williams off at her home then rung Mr James the caretaker, "Ah, Ken, it's Cerys, I need to get into the school tonight!"

Chapter Eight

Mrs Ploughy drove all the way to Newport from Tenby, (that's like 50 miles or nearly 100 miles or something, anyway it's really far!), and met the caretaker in the car park, "What's so important Mrs Ploughy?", Ken the caretaker asked, "Oh um, nothing really, I just left my lucky pen in my office!" Mrs Ploughy said quickly before rushing through the front door and promising to drop the keys back to Ken after she had finished so he could get back to his family dinner. Mrs Ploughy watched Ken drive away muttering, "Pen!! All this way for a pen!!", she then turned to face the school, "Right then, let's sort you out!".

As Mrs Ploughy walked through the door to the reception area, a puff of golden stardust engulfed her. The cloud thinned and Mrs Ploughy stood with her hands on her hips with a beautiful golden rose scented cloud circled around her like a halo; she was wearing a fantastic golden robe filled with living fairies that were all dancing on miniature stages, her hat looked like a squashed watermelon, just golden in colour.

For you see Mrs Ploughy was actually, the queen of the fairies and very magical indeed, (As well as being one fantastic teacher!) She had cast the magical spell on Dewi the dragon the day he arrived at the school and she was responsible for filling the children's lives with a little magic every day, she was also responsible for Tristyn's mum feeling faint and the rest of their day going so well, she could not risk them popping to the school or contacting Mr James themselves, she had some cleaning up to do!

Straight away Mrs Ploughy set all
her fairies to work, "As quick as
you like, my fairies take flight and

undo all this mischief for me". The
fairies flew off in all directions
each one tackling one
gymkitasaurus at a time, as they
were being caught the fairies tied
them with golden threads ready
for Mrs Ploughy to deal with.

Happy with the work her fairies
were doing, Mrs Ploughy looked
around the reception, "Hmm,
where has my dragon gone?
Dewi? Dewi Draig, where are
you?" A small whimper came from
the medical room; Mrs Ploughy
unlocked the door to find Dewi
stood facing the wall completely
stuck, "Oh Dewi! What have they

done to you?" Dog-like, Dewi tried to flip over onto his back and have his belly rubbed but he was far too big and got even more stuck! "Oh Dewi!" Mrs Ploughy chuckled, "Let's make you smaller", with one wave of her hand Dewi shrunk down to the size of a Great Dane about four-foot-high and managed to free himself, "Now be a good dragon and go and help the fairies".

As Dewi flew off to tackle the biggest gymkitasaurus, Mrs Ploughy slowly opened her office door, "I see you, you naughty little gymkitasaurus, what have you done to my office?!" All her paperwork was strewn across the floor and the walls were covered with pen marks, thank goodness gymkitasaurusi cannot spell or who knows what they would have written on the walls!!

Before it could run, Mrs Ploughy had bound it in golden thread then with the click of her finger Tristyn's gym bag appeared, "Well that's just as bad!" Mrs Ploughy turned to T gymkitasaurus and pulled on the golden rope, each section fell apart and was individually bound with more of the golden rope, T-shirt, shorts,

socks and daps each one had a
section of rope tied around it,
binding it on its own. The rope
then started to fall slowly into the
gym bag, while the green stench
cloud was engulfed by the golden
rose scented cloud that was
following Mrs Ploughy.

As Mrs Ploughy moved around the
school, the fairies handed her
gymkitasauri one after the other
and Mrs Ploughy dealt with them
all in the same way, even Mr
Thomas's gymkitasaurus got the
same treatment. Once they were
all caught, Mrs Ploughy gathered
them in the main hall and told

them off, "I do not want to have to speak to any of you again this half term, I have won our little game of cat and mouse now off you go and behave!" With an earth-shattering clap of her hands Mrs Ploughy sent all the gym bags back to their pegs where a golden bag was waiting for them, once the gym kit bags were secured inside, a magical padlock disguised as a label appeared on the front, to make sure this did not happen again.

"Right my fairies and Dewi, we need to clean up this mess, Mr James will not be very happy if we just walk away and leave the school like this, time to get to work and clean this mess away. Dewi being a dragon tried to burn all the mess away but stopped when Mrs Ploughy ran across the hall just as he was setting fire to the curtains in an attempt to get rid of the floury mess that was dripping from them like raw snot, "No Dewi, we cannot burn everything or we will have to buy all new, we need to clean this up"

Now, you may well be thinking, "Mrs Ploughy is the queen of the fairies and truly magical why doesn't she just magic the mess away and go home to watch Thunderpants and the world of underwear or other such great animated films. The reason Mrs Ploughy didn't use her magic for all of the clean up was firstly magic can leave remnants, coating all the items of the school which can make things come to life, they wouldn't do anything naughty but you can never tell when they will start playing up, can you imagine the call to the police at 2am, "Hello, a whiteboard is doing the 'cha cha' in the middle of Newcity Primary School hall with a filing cabinet, can you send someone?", "Yes Sir, we will send out the unlawful dance department right away!". Secondly it was a really good workout!

So Mrs Ploughy and the fairies all had to clean by hand while Dewi cleaned by claw, when he finally stopped trying to burn everything!

Chapter Nine

After the half term holiday, all the children ran back to their classrooms. Some found golden bags on their pegs, Tristyn was one of them, his label read; "Our school is our home, please treat it with care and wash stinky gym kits – it is only fair!"

At the end of the day Tristyn and the other children with golden bags took them home to be washed. "You see Tristyn, it is important to wash your gym kit isn't it and you have three bags of gym kit to be washed – imagine the stench!!", Mum did not think twice about what could have happened or her school that was destroyed by gymkitasaurus's, another one of Mrs Ploughy's little spells, a forget-me-for-now, mum would remember it all but once the danger had gone for good, at least this time.

As mum opened the golden bags she was engulfed by the scent of roses but very quickly the scent disappeared, and a foul stench filled its place, "Eww!! Tristyn did you really let your clothes get this stinky?", Mum cried as she stuffed the gym kits into the washing machine. The stench was another of Mrs Ploughy's little spells to ensure the gym kits were washed straight away, lots of households were being filled with the stinky pong as the gym kits were opened and washed one by one.

As the water filled the drum of the washing machine, one armless sleeve hit the inside of the door, the faceless cloud formed once again into a mouth, this time it looked as though it was shouting out, "No!!!"

As the washing powder joined the water in the machine the green gunge that has permeated the fibres of the gym kit was washed away and that was it, over.

Tristyn's gym kit was clean and T
gymkitasaurus was gone for good

...

or was he?